BEAKY BARNES and the Devious Duck

written and illustrated by
David Ezra Stein

Penguin Workshop

CAST OF CHARACTERS

BEAKY BARNES.................................an intelligent chicken
THE INVENTOR....Beaky's roommate; a lady with big ideas
INSPECTOR COBB.......... town health and safety inspector
THE CHEF .... a kindly chef
THE DUCK.....................................a tricky visitor to town
CHICKIE BARNES ....Beaky's chick
SUSANA BANDANA .... local bird lover
MR. HOPPITT E. FROGG..... Susana's friend from the park

FRESH FISH and MAURICE THE ELEPHANT .... background characters

BEAKY BARNES AND THE DEVIOUS DUCK
IS BROUGHT TO YOU BY:
CUD GUM:
The chewing gum for cows.
CUD.
How today's cows chew™
AND
BRAMSONITE LUGGAGE
When you REALLY need to get out of town, use Bramsonite Luggage.
PROFESSOR M. E. YOW

clackita clackita clackita

clackita clackita clackita clackita

HOW to FOOL people
Simpleton! This stop, Simpleton!
SIMPLETON TOWN LIMITS

WAK! WAK!
CAFÉ
I'm sorry, little duck. No money, no bread.
WAK! WAK! WAK!

Well, I'm a softy. Here's a slice.
WAK!
NUM! NUM! NUM!
FÉ
Yeesh. What a messy eater. Now get along out of here!
swiff swiff

Meanwhile . . .
Humph! No one ever does anything WRONG around here!
Well, it IS only 5 a.m.
Maybe I will go to the café for breakfast!
Here you are, Inspector. One bowl of oatmeal, extra small.
Thank you, Chef!
Whoops! You forgot the never-ending jar of molasses!
Yes, of course.

Here you are.
CLUMP!
Yum, yum!
SWIZZLE!
MR. STRAPPING MOLASSES
GLUG!
Strapping!

Let me inspect myself!
CAFÉ
OK, body! Show me STRAPPING!
HRRRR!
POP!
POP!

flump!
slump!
oh.
I guess I am not very strapping.
Nyup, nyup!
BLECH!
I love Chef, but he puts too much molasses in the oatmeal.

Meanwhile, at Beaky and Inventor's . . .
Siiip!
!
breakfast
peck!
Bye, Mama!
Bye, roomie! Have a good day at work!
Come on, Chickie! Let's get breakfast!
Whee!

Hmm, hmm!
SIMPLETON LIBRARY
STORY TIME!

I just haven't been inspired to invent anything lately.
Super Chickie!
Ahh! Chickie! Get off me! I'm trying to work!
Here, why don't you sit in your seat and eat some corn mush?
CLIP!

Unbuckle!
Chickie! No! Get back in your seat!
Hee hee hee
Great Idea Nest
Chickie! Stay out of my lab!

BWAM!!
Great Idea Nest
Oh no, Chickie! What did you do?
Come on! We are going for a walk!

CAFÉ to GO!
Good morning, Chef. Give me a cup of coffee.
Very well.
Ever since Beaky got a job at the library, I haven't gotten much inventing done.
You know, I was just thinking of you. Listen to this!
S.O.C.K. Kitchen Contest
"S.O.C.K., the Society of Chef's Kitchens" – of which I am a member – "invites you to enter your KITCHEN INVENTIONS into the kitchen invention contest!"

"Inventions should help chefs and cooks, and are due Friday. Cash prizes!"
Wow! Thanks, Chef! I'll totally enter that!
sugar
. . . If I have a chance!
CAFÉ to Go!
Come on, you! Park!

Meanwhile, in the park . . .
WAK! WAK! WAK!
Do you want some, too? Aw, what a cute little fellow. All right, here you go!
HEY! You were supposed to share!
CLOMP!
Shoo! You've had enough!
Greedy duck!

HOW to FOOL people
TRICK # 35:
SNAKE OIL
Sell fake potions to swindle people out of their money.
#34:
RUN
is to get
s car. You
ive at their
a few weeks.

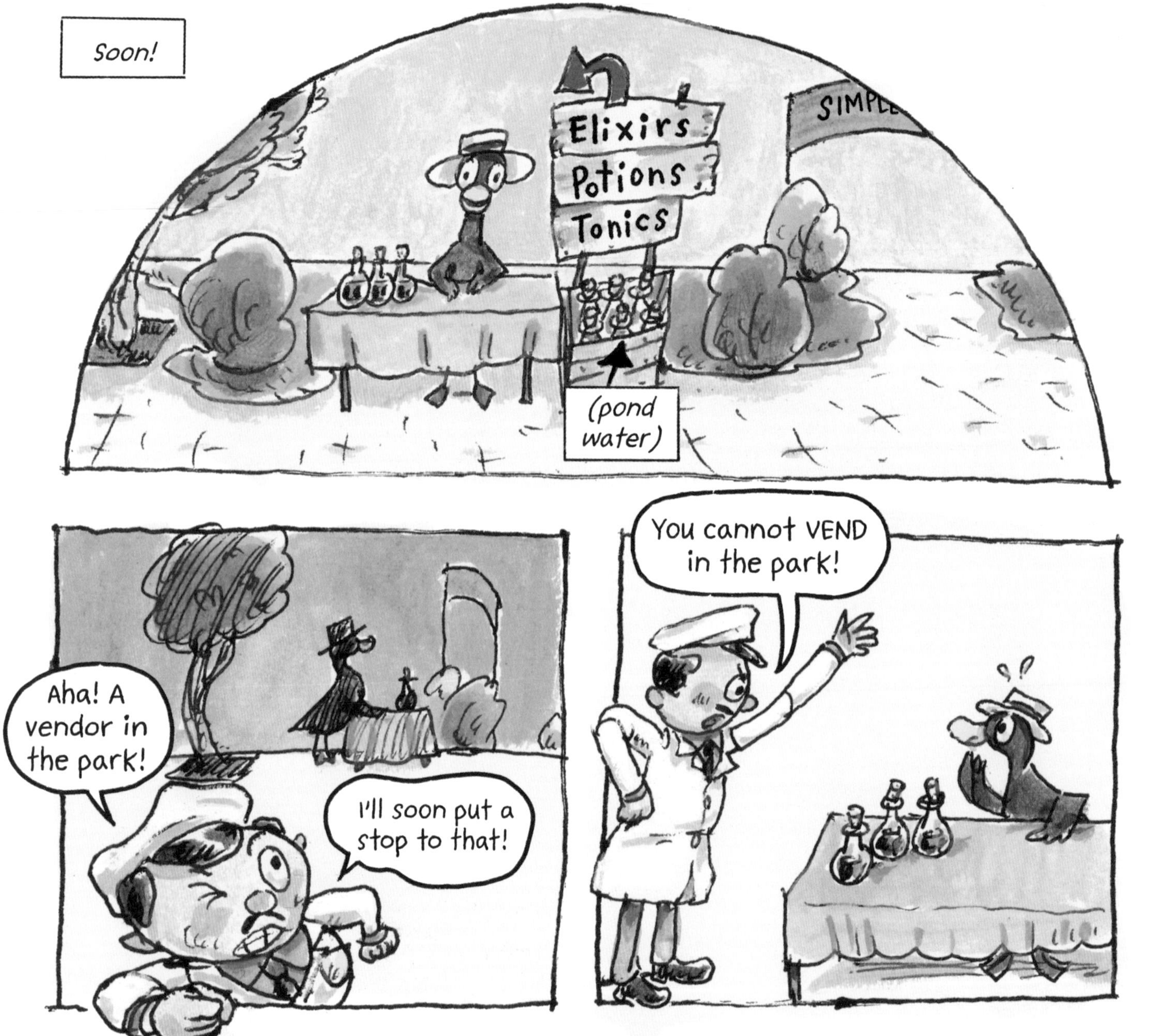
Soon!
Elixirs
Potions
Tonics
SIMPL
(pond water)
Aha! A vendor in the park!
I'll soon put a stop to that!
You cannot VEND in the park!

What is this stuff? Elixir?
Mm-hmm!
Say! You don't have . . .
. . . Any elixir of strength, do you?

Uh-huh!
ELIXIR
SQUEAK
SQUEAK
SQUEAK
ELIXIR of strength
ding!

Er, excuse me, but . . .
Could this make me . . . STRAPPING?
Uh-huh!
Happy Cry!

ADVERTISEMENT
NOT QUITE AS STRONG AS AN OX?
OX
YOU
ZING!
POW!
GET: DR. PUMPERNICKEL'S POWERSAUCE
POWER
IN THE BLACK BOTTLE THAT SMELLS OF EGGS!
POWER your day with POWERSAUCE
Note: Dr. Pumpernickel is not a real doctor. Powersauce is not real powersauce. It is pond water.

OK! Here's all my money!
Wak!
$$$
Elixir of Strength, come to Papa!
POIT!
BLEAH! It smells like low tide!

Oh well! I paid a lot of money for this elixir, so it MUST be good!
GUZZLE!
AHH! Yes! I can feel it working already!

First, I'll do a few dozen laps around the town!
Followed by five or six hundred push-ups!
Heave all these boulders!
YAH!
And push . . . this bus . . . across . . . the parking lot!
BEEEEEP!
CUD
TRY CUD!

Whew! Being strapping is a lot of work!
I must find a place to take a nap!
Here looks good!
ZZZ

Meanwhile . . .
Here you are, sir!
Would you like butter?
NOM NOM NOM!
Ew.

Z
Z

That afternoon . . .
Where am I?
GROAN! Those feats of strength! Every muscle in my body is sore!
I'm so sore, I can't open the door to my house!
clicka clicka clicka
Oh yeah – it's locked!
Hum dee dum!
CLICK

REVIEWS

DR. PUMPERNICKEL'S POWERSAUCE

Pow!

★

COBB35

STILL WIMPY

I paid a lot of money for this elixir, but now I am not strapping anymore.

☆☆☆☆☆

RANDOMDUCK3

WORKS GREAT!

I went from a measly mallard to a duck with muscles! Thank you, Dr. Pumpernickel!

☆☆☆☆

PARKFROG2

A NICE DRINK.

Tastes like mud!

Meanwhile . . .
All right, buddy! Have some snacks till we get home.
YAY!
MUNCH
MUNCH
MUNCH

Just then . . .
BAKER NEEDED
BAKER NEEDED for new bakery at the café
CAFÉ
Can't you just bake things yourself?
NO!
Just between us . . .
I am afraid of yeast!

Soon!
All right, Chickie! Here we are! Home sweet home!
AAHH! Where's Chickie?!
Wak!
Boo! Me and Ducky was hiding!
Hey! Ducky, I have a great idea: Will you watch Chickie for a bit while I make lunch?
Wak!
Yay!

Ten minutes later . . .
OK, I brought lunch for – OH NO!
Burp!
WAK!
You took all the snacks without asking!
Please leave! You're a bad influence on Chickie!
SLAM!

That evening . . .
Buck, cluck!
Welcome home, roomie!
Mama!
Whew! What a long day! What should we have for dinner?
PIZZA!

Soon!
Why does pizza always take thirty minutes to come?
Hey! That gives me an idea!
I love great ideas!
great idea notebook
instant
sudden pizza
from zero
to pizza!

ADVERTISEMENT
Uh-oh! Looks like someone's got the Dinnertime Growlies!
"Dad!"
"We're hungry!"
"For PIZZA!"
FRIENDS, HAVE YOU EVER NEEDED
PIZZA RIGHT NOW?
I'm not talking about in thirty minutes. Well, you're in luck! With
KNABCO SUDDEN PIZZA!
"No problem, kids!"
PIZZA PELLETS
Basil 'N' Cheese
drip!
Just add water!
BLAM
. . . And pizza will appear!
"Yay!"
"Pizza!"
Pizza: yay.
SUDDEN PIZZA!
Suddenly, I'm hungry™
Warning! Do not swallow pellets.

The next morning . . .
Time to exercise!

HOW to FOOL People

TRICK #57: EXERCISE EQUIPMENT
Can be very profitable. The best thing is, it doesn't even have to WORK!

Soon . . .
Paper shoes??? What?
SIMPLETO
WOW!
PAPER SHOES Latest Jogging trend
fake mustache
Ahahahahaha!
"Latest jogging trend. Almost like wearing no shoes at all!"
PAPER SHOES Latest
My shoes DO pinch sometimes!

cloud feet
Yay!
And I am a jogger! All right, I'll take them!
WOW!
$
Here you go!
Ooh! So refreshingly light!

No bag! I'll wear them home!
La la la la la!
Ooh! Look! I can even read the comics on my paper shoes!
AHA! HA! HA! That's a good one!

Meanwhile . . .
NOK, NOK!
Hi, Chef! Want to see my kitchen invention? I worked on it all night!
Sure, Ms. Inventor! Please, come in!
I've mixed ordinary dough with dynamite to make SUDDEN DOUGH!
PLUNK!
What, like INSTANT dough, you might ask?

NO! instant dough isn't fast enough for today's busy people!
STOMP!
But SUDDEN dough is ready BEFORE you even expect it!
IMAGINE! Muffins in a matter of seconds!
Pizza faster than you can blink!
I'm imagining it!
For someone like me who does not like to bake, it could be marvelous!

Simply mold the dough into the desired shape . . .
Add a single drop of water, and . . .
PLIP!
RRRUMMBLE
Hit the deck!

BAOW!

Whoaaa!
PSCCHH!
Thank you!
Don't mention it!
So! Did you notice this great pizza crust?
Mmhmm.

What do you think? Prize material?
Hmf.
flip!
KLUNK!

Please leave my restaurant.

AND DO NOT COME BACK UNTIL YOU HAVE AN INVENTION THAT DOES NOT SET MY HAT ON FIRE!!
flip!
KLUNK!
SUDDEN DOUGH
CAFÉ
That didn't go great.

Meanwhile . . .
MAJOR
MINI-MART
GROCERIES

BREAD
LONG BREAD
SUPER-LONG BREAD
free sample inside!
BREAD
BOOP!

NOM
NOM
NOM

?

Imitation ointment
KNABCO

ADVERTISEMENT
WANT TO BE ANYONE BUT YOU?
Before
After
With Copy-Catter Imitation Ointment, you can be whoever you want to be, even if you still really aren't! Simply concentrate very hard on someone you want to be and you will become them.
MEOW!
COPY-CATTER
IMITATION OINTMENT
Just look for the MEOW! on the label.
Meow!

Healthy, healthy me!
Healthy *huff, puff* me!
SQUIRT!
POP!
WAK!

!
waddle
waddle
waddle
WAK!
COBB

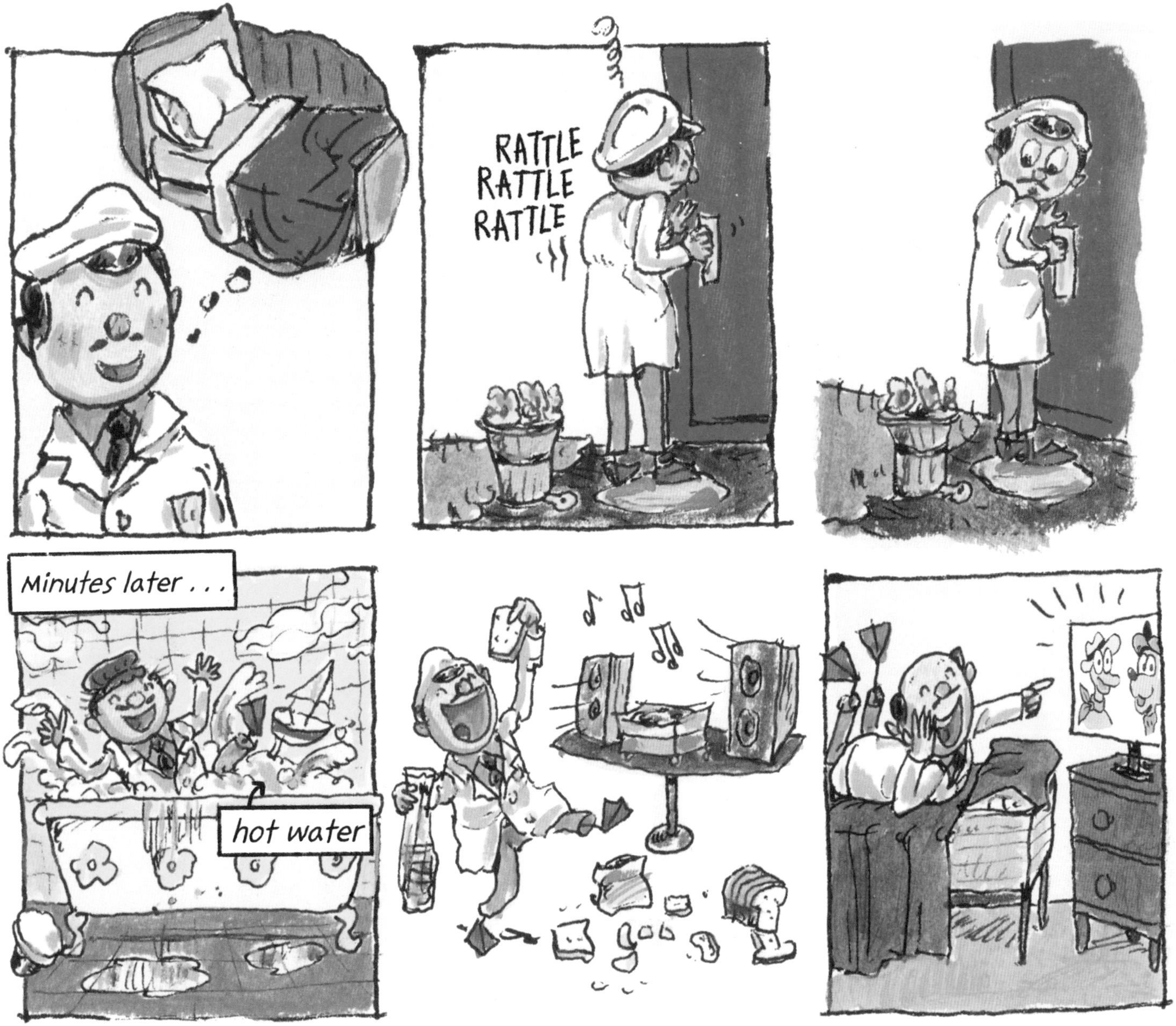
RATTLE
RATTLE
RATTLE
Minutes later . . .
hot water

Soon!
I'm home!
AIEE! I'm ALREADY home!
WAK!
BREAD
Are you really me??
WAK!
But if you're me, then who am I?

Well, Inspector! It's very nice of you to share your bread with me while I figure out who I am.
WAK!
munch munch

Wait a minute! Why do you keep quacking?
And why do you have DUCK FEET?
Rut-roh!
Not so fast, you phony me!
plop!
You're coming with me!

AHA!
What's this?
"Imitation ointment.
Washes off with cold
water."
Wait here one
second, please!
wsshh...

There!
BLOOSH!
AHA! You! I should have known.

REVIEWS

ZEFTY BRAND PAPER SHOES

★★★★★

RANDOMDUCK3

EXCELLENT QUALITY

Light as a feather. A duck feather! LOL

★

COBB35

CHANGING MY REVIEW!

From five stars to one star!
I thought these shoes were great, until I got them wet while soaking a duck. Now they're RUINED!

★★

PARKFROG2

I DON'T WEAR SHOES.

★★★★★

INVENTIN-GAL9

LOVE 'EM!

Great idea!

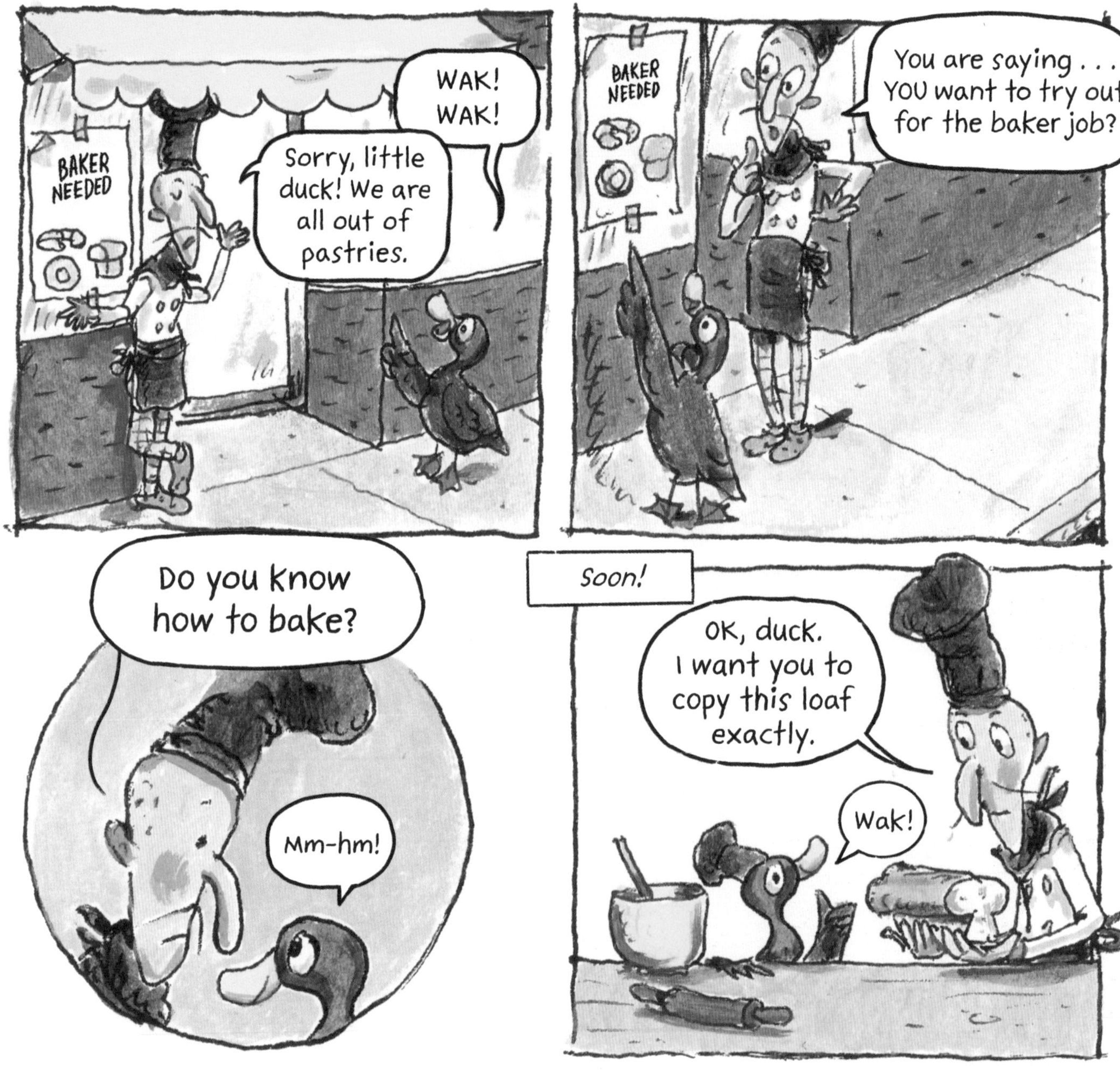
BAKER NEEDED
WAK! WAK!
Sorry, little duck! We are all out of pastries.
BAKER NEEDED
You are saying . . . YOU want to try out for the baker job?
Do you know how to bake?
Mm-hm!
Soon!
OK, duck. I want you to copy this loaf exactly.
Wak!

You have forty-five minutes. On your mark, get set, GO!
NOM NOM NOM
BAKER NEEDED

SIMPLETON
LIBRARY
INFORMATION
Wak?

INFORMATION
Buck, cluck!
SCAMS, A-J
SCAMS, K-
READ
SCAMS
more scams
She sells scams by the seashore
scams for fun and PROFIT
SON OF SCAMS
PRO TIP:
LEARN WHAT PEOPLE REALLY WANT, AND SELL IT TO THEM.
IP:
ELPS
LATTER
VICTIM.

Later that night . . .
How's the baker search going, Chef?
Terribly.
If only I was a good baker myself!
My Nana was a wonderful baker! Her cheesecake was DELICIOUS!
I miss that cheesecake!

I just can't get it to come out right! It tastes like GLUE!
My Aunt Tillie makes a peach pie so good, you could eat the whole thing at once!
Did you ever have an ice-cream sandwich with chocolate chip cookies for the sandwich part? So good!
You guys should try my brother's bug biscuits! YUM!

Me? I miss the doughnut they gave me when I first became an inspector. It was a jelly doughnut with a big ribbon on it!
Heh heh!

The next morning . . .
SIMPLETON LIBRARY
Bye, roomie! Have a good day at work!
Hee hee! These paper shoes I bought are so light!
Hee hee!
WHEE! It's like I don't weigh anything at all!
WHEE!
HEY! That gives me a great idea.
KEEP OFF

ADVERTISEMENT
HEY, YOU!
Want to eat PIES, COOKIES, DOUGHNUTS, and CAKE that will simply
LIFT
you off your feet?
Just bake them with:
KNABCO
HELIUM
DOUGH
The only dough that makes you
DEFY GRAVITY!
KNABCO: What a Great Idea!™

Soon!
Chef! Chef! Guess what? I have the kitchen idea of the CENTURY!
Yes?
Here it is! No, that's Chickie.
Hi!
For thousands of years, people have wanted to fly like birds!
True.
Well, what if there was a way to float in the air just by eating baked goods?
No! You're kidding. That would be quite marvelous!

TA-DA! Helium dough!
Look at this batch of muffins! If you ate this whole batch, do you know what would happen?
Your feet would leave the ground!
Hold on, Ms. Inventor! How can it be possible, what you say?
BECAUSE each muffin is INFUSED with HELIUM! It makes you go UP!
Ooh!
Egads! And the FLAVOR? How is it?
Pretty tasty! Please try for yourself! It's perfectly safe. I spent all night testing it!
Nom, nom. Hmm, not bad.

Wow! I feel so incredibly light!
mouse voice
HEY! What is the matter with my voice?
Why am I so squeaky??
Gosh! It must be a side effect of the helium! I'm so sorry, I –
OUT!

The next morning . . .
DR. WEBBERLY'S
FOOD SÉANCES*
BRING BACK LOST FOODS YOU LOVED.
*SAY-on-siz

ADVERTISEMENT
DO YOU MISS A REALLY DELICIOUS FOOD OR DESSERT BECAUSE YOU ALREADY ATE IT?
YOU NEED
DOCTOR WEBBERLY'S
FOOD SÉANCES
ALL GONE
NO MORE
DOCTOR W.

ADVERTISEMENT
"Where does food go when you eat it?" a bright young nipper might ask. Well . . .
REAL WORLD
GREAT BEYOND
OVERLAP
You
Grandma Rachel's nut muffins
It is in this overlap between worlds that we can visit with past goodies, say hello, and get news from the Great Beyond!
ADVERTISEMENT. NOT TRUE AT ALL.

ADVERTISEMENT
Speak, ice cream! How are they treating you "over there"?
Verryy wellll! It's always 32 degrees heeerrre!
ACTUAL SÉANCE
Doctor W. will reunite YOU with a long-lost treat!
NOTE: NOT TRUE.

WOW
Food Séance tonight at DUSK
At the old abandoned shack.
DR. WEBBERLY'S
FOOD SÉANCES
BACK LOST FOODS
YOU LOVED.
SO! Planning a séance, eh?
Mm-hmm!

Ha! Ever since I laid eyes on you, I knew you were the type to have a séance!
And now I have only ONE question for you!
What is a séance??
Psychics
Séance
In a séance, a spirit guide or medium can speak to the dead.
Oh.

I see!
At a food séance, you can talk to a food you really miss!
Do you think my first doughnut is out there somewhere, waiting to talk to me?
Mm-hmm!
COBB
In that case, I'll sign up!
I want to talk to my ice-cream sandwich!
My brother's bug biscuits!
Nana's cheesecake!

Meanwhile . . .
BAMP! BAMP! BAMP!
CHECKOUT
!
Notice! Someone borrowed the following books at your library using a FAKE library card!
Scams, by J. L. McGillicuddy,
More Scams, by Sneaky Sandra,
Summer Scams, by G. Cunningham,
She Sells Scams by the Seashore . . .
CHECKOUT
Wak!
SIMPLETON LIBRARY

That night . . .
Séance Here TONIGHT
I'm so excited!
Me too!
Doughnut, here I come!
TONIGHT
CREEAAK!
Oh my gosh! Something's happening!
Let's go in! I'm not afraid! That's why I'm back here!
Welcome, spirit seekers. Please have a seat. The medium will see you one by one.

Qua ha ha!
OUIJA BOARD

Meanwhile . . .
Oh! I can't believe I'm missing the séance!
But the kitchen contest deadline is tomorrow! I need ideas! Let's see what I have in my notebook . . .
flip
flip
Exploding stuff . . . too dangerous. Glow in the dark! No one cooks in the dark.
Hi!
Not now, Chickie! Go play, please!

Mama's out chasing some library bad guy, and I need to do this before your bath!
ok.
Hey! What about this! Sour and spicy muffins! That's kind of a great idea!
I bet no one's ever thought of THAT before!

ADVERTISEMENT
HOWDY, PARDNER!
ARE YOU SICK of SWEET, SAVORY MUFFINS??
blueberry
banana nut
Blech! Am I right?
GET YOURSELF A PACK OF KNABCO
SOUR
+
SPICY
MUFFINS
WITH SOUR TO WAKE YOU UP,
AND SPICY TO GET YOU GOING!

OK! Time to do some quick baking. Then maybe I can still get to the séance.
Chickie bakes, too!
whippa whippa whippa
Great, Chickie! Just use your play dough.
Chickie makes cookies!
Helium Dough
Helium Dough

Now Chickie EATS the cookies!
Helium Dough *Just add water
Yum! Salty!
BLOOP!
Uh-oh!

Hi, Auntie!
Just one second, sweetie! Let's see how Chef likes THESE! Ooh, hot!
Let these cool by the open window!
ZIP!

There! Now what can I do for you, Chickie?
Oh my gosh! Where's Chickie??

Hee hee hee!
Whee!
No, Mama! Help!

Meanwhile . . .
$$$
Qua ha ha!
Qua ha ha!
Huh?

TIP: Whatever happens, do not give up on a scam once it starts, or there will be BIG TROUBLE!
HOW to FOOL
toss
PBBT!
What is THIS? Why are you giving the money back?
Aren't we having a séance?
Hey! Come back! I want to talk to my DOUGHNUT!

Aha!
Books
!
GIVE
Oh, Beaky! It's terrible! I can't find Chickie!
I demand to talk to my doughnut!
Mama! Help!
Oh my gosh! There he is! He's floating away!
Hey! That's not safe!

He must've eaten the helium dough!
Buck, cluck!
Floating away is against the rules!!
FWEET!
Hey! The duck! He's trying to save Chickie!
flap flap flap
Wak!
Ducky! Help!
It's no use! They're not heavy enough!

If only I could fly! I'd soar up there, and –
Trip!
Whoop!
Meanwhile . . .
YEAAAARRGHH!
BOOF!

Ooh, look! I can see the ducky from here. Hi, Ducky!
imitation ointment
SQUIRT!
What doing, Ducky?
POP!
QUAAAAAAAAK!

Meanwhile . . .
Maybe I should get up. There doesn't seem to be anything broken.
NEEEYOW
BOOF!
OW! What hit me?
Oh! You're me!
Wak!

Chickie's safe! We did it! I did it!
Good job, me! Ya big lug!
Wak!
I guess we were the right person for the job!
splash splash!
You are handsome, you know that? Hey! What are you doing?
POOF!
Wak!

Ah, well. I guess there's only room for one Cobb, anyway!
Hi, Mama!
Buck, cluck!
Oh, Chickie! You're OK!
Cannonball Cobb to the rescue!
Yup! I saved the day! Did you see the way I –
Duck! You were so brave! And smart.
Buck, cluck!
Ahem! What about me?

You were brave, too, Inspector!
PAT PAT
Hold on tight for a while, till the helium wears off.
I didn't have to be strapping to be a hero!
Hey! Wait up!

The next morning . . .
INFORMATION
SCAMS
SON OF SCAMS
Soon . . .
JOBS/CAREERS
Ahem!
BAKING
ZIP!

Some days later . . .
BAKER NEEDED
CA
Sigh.
CAFÉ
Oh no! Not YOU again!
I am sorry.
Please give me a second chance.
Oh, OK! I am a softy. Let's see what you can do.

swizzle
BRRZZHH!!
pour!
fwsssh!

Tick
tock
Tick
tock
Tick
tock
tic
tic
tic
tic
BZZZ!
Ta-da!

Mmm!
Ahem!
ZIP!

This is good!
You are hired!
Qua-hoo!
CAFÉ
RIP!
CAFÉ
Buck, cluck!

Early the next morning . . .
CAFÉ
CAFÉ
WHIZZZ!
WHIZZZZZZ!
SCOOP

WAK! WAK!
For me?
Oh, what's this?
Wak! Wak!
whew.
Thanks, Duck!

you Are Cordially Invited
to the

GRAND OPENING

of the

CAFÉ BAKERY COUNTER

with

desserts & treats by the Duck,
our new baker.

some of the treats

Soon!
Wow! Everything looks so yummy!
GRAND OPENING
Step right up! Do not be shy! Here is our new menu, just printed last night!
Goodies!
All this needs INSPECTION!
HEY! Wait a minute! "Nana's Cheesecake"! "Cobb's Jelly Doughnut"! "Frogg's Bug Biscuits"! These are our favorite recipes!
MENU
Duck, what a wonderful idea!

This ice-cream sandwich is so good!
I feel like a new inspector!
COBB
These bugs are nice and crispy! Just like I like 'em!
Nana, you would be proud!

VZZZZZZ!
VZZZZZZZZZZ
Goodness gracious! Ms. Inventor, what is THAT?
Oh, it's just the CRUMB SUCKER 3000, my tabletop cleaning device!
Well, it's genius! I'll take ten of them for my new bakery!
THE END

HOW
to
FOOL